Before reading

Look at the book cover
Ask, "What do you think

To build independence,
at the start of this book. .... practice, turn
back to pages 6 and 7 in 11a and read the words again with
the child.

During reading

Offer plenty of support and praise as the child reads the story.
Listen carefully and respond to events in the text.

In **11c**, the new **Key Words** are not shown at the bottom of
the page. If the child hesitates over a word, turn to the back
of the book to practise reading it together. If the word is
phonically decodable, you can sound out the letters and
blend the sounds to read the word ("d-o-g, dog"). Praise the
child for their effort, then return to the story.

Pause every few pages and ask questions to check the child's
understanding of what they have read. If they begin to lose
concentration, stop reading and save the page for later.

Celebrate the child's achievement and come back to the
story the next day.

After reading

After reading this book, ask, "Did you enjoy the story? What did
you like about it?" Encourage the child to share their opinions.

Use the comprehension questions on page 54 to check the
child's understanding and recall of the text.

Ladybird

Series Consultant: Professor David Waugh
With thanks to Kulwinder Maude

LADYBIRD BOOKS

UK | USA | Canada | Ireland | Australia
India | New Zealand | South Africa

Ladybird Books is part of the Penguin Random House group of companies
whose addresses can be found at global.penguinrandomhouse.com.
www.penguin.co.uk   www.puffin.co.uk   www.ladybird.co.uk

Original edition of Key Words with Peter and Jane first published by Ladybird Books Ltd 1964
Series updated 2023
This book first published 2023
001

Text copyright © Ladybird Books Ltd, 1964, 2023
Illustrations by Martyn Cain
Based on characters and design by Gustavo Mazali
Illustrations copyright © Ladybird Books Ltd, 2023

With thanks to Liz Pemberton for her contributions in advising on the illustrations
With thanks to Inclusive Minds for connecting us with their Inclusion Ambassador network,
and in particular thanks to Guntaas Kaur Chugh for her input on the illustrations

Printed in China

The authorized representative in the EEA is Penguin Random House Ireland,
Morrison Chambers, 32 Nassau Street, Dublin D02 YH68

A CIP catalogue record for this book is available from the British Library

ISBN: 978-0-241-51105-3

All correspondence to:
Ladybird Books
Penguin Random House Children's
One Embassy Gardens, 8 Viaduct Gardens, London SW11 7BW

MIX
Paper from
responsible sources
FSC® C018179

Key Words

with Peter and Jane

11c

The lost sheep

Based on the original
Key Words with Peter and Jane
reading scheme and research by William Murray

Original edition written by William Murray
This edition written by Abbie Rushton
Illustrated by Martyn Cain
Based on characters and design by Gustavo Mazali

It was the weekend, and Peter and Jane were going on an adventure to Pippa's farm. Dad drove them there through the countryside.

"Do you think Pippa has picked a name for her new kitten yet?" asked Peter.

"Peter! Jane!" Pippa cried. "It was so long ago that you last came around!"

"It's only been two weeks," Jane said, laughing.

"We have made cakes," said Pippa. "They took a while to make, so I hope you like them."

"Hello! Come through," said Pippa's mum, Anna.

"Can we have some of your cake, please?" asked Peter.

"Oh, it's two cakes!" Anna said. "Pippa's dad and I need a new cake to sell in the farm cafe, so we each came up with new ideas. You're going to pick the best one."

Pippa's Dad, Matt, came over. "Hello, everyone," he said. "I can't stop for long. I need to fix a gate while it's not raining. But first, let's pick the best cake!"

"Nothing's better than lemon cake,"
said Peter.

"Just you wait," said Matt with a wink.

Peter watched while Pippa cut the other cake. "Wow, a rainbow cake!" he said.

Dad took a bite of the rainbow cake. "Oh my goodness!" he cried. "This is the best cake in the world."

"I like the lemon cake," said Peter.

"Jane, you need to pick one too,"
said Pippa.

"I do like the rainbow cake," Jane said.

"Yes!" Matt cried. "I made that one. My cake wins."

Suddenly, a small kitten ran up to them. "Meg!" Pippa cried.

"Oh! You used the name I liked for the kitten," said Peter.

The kitten ran around, then she went to play with Peter's trainers. Everyone laughed.

"That's not a toy, Meg!" said Peter.

Dad looked at his watch. "I'd better head back to the city. See you all in the morning!" he said. "Thanks for the cake."

Everyone went outside to watch Dad drive away. The children ran to the farm gate and waved.

Suddenly, Matt shouted, "I need to go too. The police just called. We may have lost some sheep."

"Oh no!" Pippa cried. "Can we come?"

"Yes, hop in," Matt said.

Everyone got in the car. Sweep, Pippa's dog, jumped in too.

They went down a country lane. "I bet they got through that hole in the gate," said Matt. "I was going to fix it today."

"Last time, the sheep went a long way away," Pippa told Peter and Jane. "It took a while to find them."

After a while, they came to a small house. The garden was full of sheep. They were eating all the plants!

Everyone jumped out of the car. The police were in the garden, and the woman who lived in the house was watching the sheep.

"Oh no! I'm so sorry," Matt said to the woman. "I came around as soon as the police called."

"It's fine," the woman said. "These things happen in the countryside. I've been watching the police run after them!"

The policeman came over. He was panting after running around after the sheep.

"Are these your lost sheep?" he asked. "They've had a big adventure!"

"Yes," Matt began. "My dog, Sweep, will run around and get them."

"We can help too," Pippa said. The children picked up the pots and the bird table.

Matt looked up at the sky. "We need to be quick. It'll rain soon."

Matt used his whistle, and Sweep ran around the garden, rounding up the sheep.

Peter loved watching Sweep as she ran around. She listened to every order from Matt.

At last, all the sheep were in the trailer behind Matt's car.

"That's so clever!" Peter said. "Could you teach me to use a whistle?"

"You can help me with the sheep later, if you like," Matt said.

"Yes, please!" cried Peter.

Matt thanked the police and said sorry to the woman again.

"I hope they didn't eat too many of your plants," Matt said. "Please come to our farm cafe this afternoon for some free tea and homemade cake!"

The woman smiled and said, "I will, thank you."

They were about to get in the car, when Jane suddenly shouted, "Wait!"

Everyone stopped. "Listen," said Jane. "I think I can hear one last lost sheep."

"I thought Sweep had rounded them all up," Matt said, frowning.

Everyone listened for a while, but there was nothing – only the first few pattering raindrops. Then, there was a small crying sound.

"It's through here," Peter cried, peering between two plants. "Oh no! I think it's hurt."

Matt lifted up the small sheep. "We need to call the vet, Pippa," he said.

The sheep sat on the children's laps while they drove back up the long country lane.

"Poor lost sheep," Pippa said softly. "Your big adventure didn't end well."

Back at the farm, Matt called the vet.

"How long do you think she'll be?" Pippa said.

"She came around quickly last time we called her," Anna said.

Peter played with the kitten while Anna made some food. Meg ran around the living room with a small toy mouse. Everyone watched as Peter had a tug of war with Meg using her toy fox.

"Ow!" Peter shouted when Meg nipped him.

"She's only playing," Pippa said, laughing.

Suddenly, the doorbell rang.

Pippa went to the door, and the vet came through. "I hear your sheep had an adventure and ran all around the countryside!" she said.

The vet sat down and took out her tools. "I just need to look at you," she said softly to the sheep.

Everyone watched while the vet checked over the little sheep. At long last, she said, "It's nothing too bad. Keep her inside tonight, and give her some food."

"Oh, thank goodness!" Anna cried.

Anna thanked the vet before she left, then everyone had lunch.

"Vets are the best," Jane said. "I'd love to be a vet and work in the countryside."

"Oh, great!" Matt said. "We always need a vet around here."

"Listen to this idea," Pippa said. "Our lost sheep ate that woman's plants. Why don't we fill a box with gifts for her?"

"Great idea," said Matt. "There's nothing in the world better than a homemade gift."

"We can give her lots of food and a plant too," Anna added.

After lunch, they went to the farm shop. Pippa found a small box they could use.

"I love seeing all the food in your shop!" Jane cried, looking at all the fruit and jars of jam.

Anna helped them to pick the best tomatoes and carrots. They added a small plant and two cartons of eggs.

"We can give the woman this food and plant if she comes here this afternoon," Anna said.

A waiter ran through from the cafe. "We've suddenly had a lot of food orders," he said to Anna. "Could you give me a hand, please?"

"We'll help too," Peter said.

They all put on aprons, then Jane took out two bits of cake on a tray.

"Oh, hello again," said the woman at the table.

It was the woman from the house where they found the sheep!

Anna came through from the shop and gave the woman the gift they had made.

"You didn't need to do that!" the woman said. "Thank you! I love the plant, and the food looks great. Your sheep did have an adventure as they ran around my garden. My name's Jess, by the way."

Anna smiled and said, "My name's Anna. Would you like the children to show you around the farm after your cake?"

"I'd love that!" said Jess.

Everyone helped in the cafe, then
Peter, Jane and Pippa showed Jess
and her friend around the farm.
Pippa led everyone up the farm track.

"We can show you the horses, Jess,"
said Peter.

"Great idea," Pippa said. "Let's give
them some food."

When they reached the horses, Jess
patted the long, soft nose of one of them.

"His name is Merlin," Pippa told Jess.
"We've had him for a while – since
I was two. That smaller one is named
Bella. We've only had her for around
three months."

Next, they went to see the chickens.
The chickens were in a pen to keep
out foxes.

"Can you remember all their names?"
Pippa asked Jane.

"Er . . ." Jane said, looking around.
There were so many chickens!

"I'm only joking," Pippa said, laughing.
"This one's name is Sky."

"Shall we show Jess the cows too?"
asked Jane.

Matt was in the cow barn.

"I need to round up the sheep next.
Do you want to come, Peter?" he asked.

"Oh, yes please!" said Peter.

41

Peter and Matt went out with Sweep.

Matt had two whistles. Peter took one, then Matt gave two long, sharp blasts with his whistle. Sweep went to the sheep. Then, Matt made another sound, and Sweep ran round to the left of the sheep.

"Now, you do it," Matt said. "Toot your whistle with one long blast."

Peter blew the whistle. It worked! He watched as Sweep suddenly lay down.

"Good work!" Matt cried.

Sweep ran back and forth, rounding up the sheep.

43

Then, Peter and Matt went back to the farmhouse, just as the sun set in the sky.

"How about a walk before dinner?" Anna asked the children.

"Oh, yes!" they cried.

"We'll need to put on thicker clothes and raincoats," Matt said.

Everyone went out into the dark night. They went through the woods, using two torches so they could see the way.

"Look up, everyone," Matt said. "We're in luck tonight. It's raining again, but you can still see stars in the sky."

Peter told everyone the names of some stars in the night sky.

"The sky is so big that it makes me feel small," said Pippa.

"Did you know that people around the world see different stars in the sky?" Peter said.

"Really?" Pippa said. "Oh, look! Bats!"

They watched while bats swooped through the trees.

47

Anna said, "We need to turn the torches off now, so we don't scare the animals."

"What an adventure!" Peter said softly.

Suddenly, they saw something small run by. "What was that, Pippa?" Jane asked.

"Nothing big. Only a mouse," Pippa said.

Just then, they heard the flapping of wings. "Listen! That sounds like an owl," Matt said.

"I bet it went after that mouse," Jane said.

They kept listening and, soon, they could hear an owl's call.

Everyone walked on through the dark woods.

Stopping suddenly, Pippa said, "Listen!"

She went through a small gap between two trees.

"I've no idea what that was. There's nothing there now," Pippa said.

"It's great to have an adventure in the animals' night-time world," Jane said. "Wait . . . What's that?"

Anna used her torch, and they saw some tracks in the mud.

"A fox made these," Pippa said.

"A fox!" cried Peter. "I love foxes."

Anna looked at her watch. "Right, everyone," she began, "we should head back for some food."

Everyone went back the way they came. Then, suddenly, the three children stopped. Standing before them was . . . a big deer! As quick as a flash, it turned and ran off through the trees and into the night.

Everyone looked around in surprise, saying, "Wow!"

"This has been the best night ever!" Peter cried.

Answer these questions about
the story.

1 What kind of cakes have Pippa's
family baked? Why have they
baked them?

2 Why do the police call Pippa's dad?

3 What does the vet tell Pippa's mum
about the small sheep?

4 Why do you think the children fill a
box with gifts for Jess?

5 What does Peter learn to do with
Pippa's dog?

6 How do you think the children feel
when they see the big deer on their
night walk?